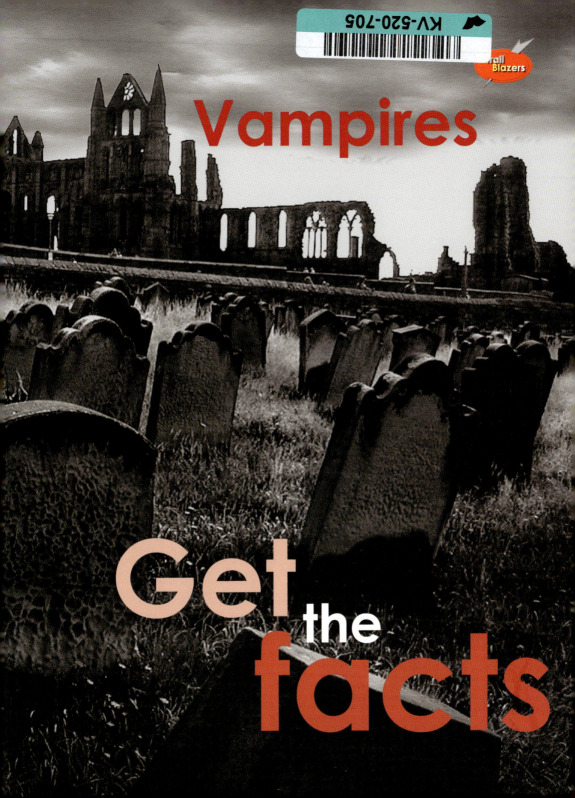

Vampires

Get the facts

What is a vampire?

Legends say that some people turn into vampires after they have died.

The vampire will come out of its grave and drink people's blood.

The vampire may even turn into an animal!

How do people become vampires?

Here are some ideas:

- by being **bitten** by a vampire
- if a **black cat** crossed your mother's path
- *even* - if you had **red hair**!

How would you know that a dead person had become a vampire?

Dig them up.

If their body was still fresh, or had moved in its coffin, or had blood on its mouth, it was a **vampire**.

Vampires

by David Orme

Ransom

Trailblazers

Vampires
by David Orme
Educational consultant: Helen Bird

Illustrated by Øivind Hovland

Published by Ransom Publishing Ltd.
51 Southgate Street, Winchester, Hants. SO23 9EH
www.ransom.co.uk

ISBN   978 184167 692 0

First published in 2009

Illustrations copyright © 2009 Øivind Hovland
'Get the Facts' section - images copyright: Bran castle, Brasov, Romania - Aurelian Gogonea; shadowy figure - Florea Marius Catalin; mirror - Michal Rozanski; lantern - Adam Gryko; garlic - Jorge Farres Sanchez; stake - Bonnie Jacobs; red-eyed face - Eva Serrabassa; Dracula illustrations - Mark Stay, Anton Brand; leech - Shizhao; assassin bug - Ira Eskins; bedbug - U.S. Center for Disease Control and Prevention; bedbug (slide) - Adam Cuerden; black pudding - Dave White; Christel Death - Renee Lee; vampire monster - Ian Knox; cemetery - Linda Bucklin; Nosferatu - Kristen Johansen; Whitby Dracula country - James Nader; girl with red hair - Simon Podgorsek.

A CIP catalogue record of this book is available from the British Library.

Vampires

Contents

So what should you do?

Fix them to their coffin with nails or a stake, so they can't escape!

Case study: a vampire from Serbia

Peter Plogojowitz died in 1725 in the country that is now **Serbia**.

Then other people started to die suddenly. Before they died, some of them said that they had been strangled by Plogojowitz.

His body was dug up and found to be fresh. A stake was put through his heart and the body was burnt.

The ruler of the region didn't believe in vampires. She made digging up bodies a crime. After this, vampire stories stopped.

Dracula

The most famous vampire story is **Dracula**.

This novel was written over 100 years ago by **Bram Stoker**. The story is partly set in Dracula's spooky castle in **Transylvania** (In Romania) and partly in England.

Bran Castle in **Romania**. This is supposed to be the real **Dracula's Castle**!

Is it? Er – no.

Whitby in **Yorkshire** – in the story, this was where Dracula arrived in England.

Van Helsing

A very important character in the story is **Van Helsing**, the vampire hunter.

This is Van Helsing's vampire hunting kit.

Lantern (Vampires don't like light. Also useful for finding your way in spooky graveyards).

Flask of water (Vampires can't cross running water, so you are safe – until the water runs out).

Garlic (They hate the stuff).

A mirror (Useful for spotting vampires – they don't have a reflection).

Stake and hammer (To finish them off).

The real Dracula?

Some people say that Dracula was based on a **real person**.

This was **Vlad Tepes**, also known as **Vlad the Impaler** and **Vlad Dracul**. He lived in Romania from 1431 to 1476.

Vlad was not a vampire. But he was very bloodthirsty!

These stories are told about Vlad:

 He stuck sharpened wooden stakes through his enemies – thousands of them!

 He would burn people to death as entertainment while he was eating dinner.

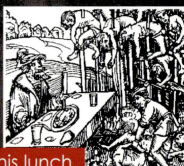

Vlad enjoying his lunch.

 If he didn't like his visitors, he would nail their hats to their heads!

 He drank their blood.

Are these stories true?

Most of these stories were made up by his enemies –

so what do you think?

Even so, he probably wasn't a person you would want to invite home for tea!

Was Dracula based on him?

Bram Stoker knew a lot about the history of Romania, and he would have known about **Vlad Dracul**.

He probably just borrowed the name. **Count Devil** is a good name for a vampire.

Dracul means dragon or devil.

Vampire bats

Vampire bats are found in Central and South America.

There are three types of vampire bat:

- Common vampire bat
- White-winged vampire bat
- Hairy-legged vampire bat

These animals feed by sucking blood from other creatures.

Their teeth are specially designed to snip through fur then cut through skin.

White-winged vampire bat

There is a chemical in their saliva (spit) to stop the animal's blood from clotting while they are drinking it. This chemical is called draculin.

Common vampire bat

I WONDER WHERE THEY GOT THAT NAME FROM?

Do vampire bats attack humans?

Sometimes. Though they don't suck blood from the neck like a vampire!

Their favourite place is the big toe!

Is it dangerous to be the victim of a vampire bat?

Yes. These bats often carry a disease called rabies. This can be fatal to animals and humans if it is not treated quickly.

Vampire bats – amazing fact

Vampire bats need to feed at least every two days.

If they can't get blood, other vampire bats will help out by sharing the blood they have collected.

More bloodsuckers

Many **insects**, such as mosquitoes, bed bugs, ticks, fleas and mites, feed on blood.

A bed bug.

Assassin bugs grab hold of their victims (usually other insects) and inject a **strong poison** into them through a tube. This poison turns their victims' insides into mush. The bugs then use the tube to **suck out the insides** – a tasty meal!

Assassin bugs are a serious threat to humans. Each year around 21,000 people die from a disease spread by these bugs.

Leeches are found in water. They attach themselves to animals (or people) and start to suck blood.

These clever creatures inject an **anaesthetic** into their victims – so the victims don't notice they are there!

A **leech**.

Lampreys live by sucking the blood from larger fish.

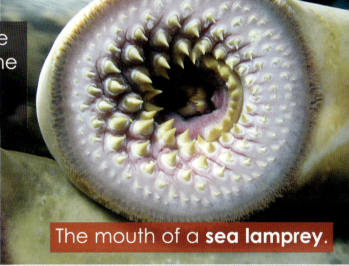

The mouth of a **sea lamprey**.

You don't have to be a vampire to enjoy blood. It can be part of the human diet too!

Black pudding – made from blood.

15

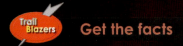

Are vampires real?

NO. So why did people believe in them, then?

Sometimes people get together and start panicking about things.

At one time, people believed that witches could cast spells and do harm to the places where they lived. There were even laws passed to deal with them.

Many people were killed because people accused them of being witches.

A witch being burned in 1531.

More recently, people have believed that they might get abducted by **aliens**.

But aliens don't exist!

But why vampires?

One reason was that people didn't understand what happened to people's bodies after they died.

Sometimes, hair and nails can keep growing.

Bodies can swell up, looking as if they have just eaten a meal. Blood can leak from the mouth of a body.

These things might make people think that a body is a vampire. Once people believe things like that, imagination takes over.

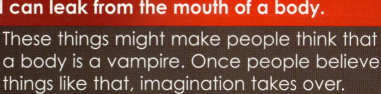

In January 2005, there was **panic** in part of Birmingham, U.K., because people thought there was a **vampire** on the loose. (There wasn't.)

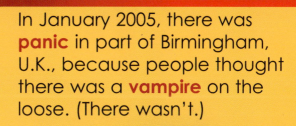

Human beings are great at believing impossible things. That's why we enjoy vampire stories!

17

Blood

In My
Eyes

Chapter 1:
A letter

I got a letter from Peter today.

Romania, Tuesday.

Dear James,

I need help! Can you come? The people in the local village are terrified of a vampire they say lives in a local castle. I don't think I can deal with this alone.

Please hurry!

Peter.

I knew I had to go. I packed my bags and set off for Romania that evening.

Peter had a room at the village inn. The castle he told me about was ten miles away in the forest.

The evening I arrived, we sat in the inn and listened to the locals. They told us that a hundred years ago, a vampire had lived in the castle. He would turn into a bat and fly down to the village. He would suck blood from the villagers.

They were sure that the vampire had returned!

Chapter 2:
The track through the forest

We were told that many people in the village had become sick. Peter and I visited some of them. Peter was sure it was the work of a vampire.

This wasn't true, of course. The village was poor, and it was clear that the sickness was caused by too much work and not enough food.

But I didn't say anything to Peter. He was enjoying himself too much!

That evening, Peter got together the things he needed to destroy a vampire. We hired horses from the village and set off into the forest.

It was a dark, lonely ride along that forest track. None of the locals dared be out after dark. Sometimes, we heard the howling of wolves away to the north.

It was midnight when we reached the castle – a dark ruin, black against the stars.

Chapter 3:
The castle

The castle roof had fallen in years before. No one could live there now. Peter had an old map of the castle. He shone his lantern on it.

'The vampire won't be inside the castle,' he said. 'Look! The map shows a tomb just here! That's where we'll find him!'

The tomb was covered in ivy and was hard to find. It had a wooden door, but it was rotten and easy to break down.

Inside the tomb there were shelves of rotting coffins. They looked as if they had been there for hundreds of years.

One of the coffins was much bigger than the others.

'That will be the one!' said Peter.

'Take care, Peter!' I said. 'You may be in great danger!'

But Peter would not listen to my warning.

Chapter 4:
The vampire

First, Peter set out the things he had brought with him – a wooden stake, a hammer, an iron bar and a jar of water.

He hung garlic around his neck. He gave me some, but I wouldn't wear it – I couldn't stand the smell of the stuff.

Peter attacked the coffin. The rotten lid broke into pieces. Peter looked inside – and groaned in disappointment.

In the coffin was a skeleton. This was no vampire!

While Peter was bending over, looking into the coffin, I took my chance. I had felt my teeth growing, growing all evening.

Grabbing Peter, I forced them into his neck. He struggled at first, but then the blood loss made him faint.

I lifted out the skeleton. This coffin would do well for me. Peter could have one of the smaller ones.

I had returned home at last.

Vampires word check

abducted	mosquitoes
anaesthetic	rabies
assassin bug	Romania
bloodsucker	skeleton
bloodthirsty	stake
chemical	strangled
coffin	tomb
Dracula	Transylvania
draculin	Van Helsing
garlic	victim
impaled	Vlad the Impaler
lamprey	Whitby
lantern	witch
leech	Yorkshire
legend	